# DEMAIN PUBLISHING

Short Sharp Shocks!

Murder! Mystery! Mayhem!

Beats! Ballads! Blank Verse!

Weird! Wonderful! Other Worlds

Horror Novels & Novellas

Science Fiction Novels & Novellas

The 'A QUIET APOCALYPSE' Series

General Fiction

Science Fiction Collections

Horror Fiction Collections

Anthologies

Audios

# Reviews for *Sister Cilice*

(First featured in the *Hellbound Hearts* Anthology, 2009)

*Sister Cilice* topped <u>Dread Central</u>'s list of the 8 most gruesome **Hellraiser** stories told outside the movies:

"Barbie Wilde's short story from the **Hellbound Hearts** anthology is one of the major standouts of that collection. It's no surprise, of course, as Wilde played the Female Cenobite in **Hellraiser II**. She clearly knows what it's like to spend time in a Cenobite's skin. This story, in fact, serves as an origin for her character. And it's both one of the best stories in the book as well as one of the most disturbing. Sister Cilice is a nun and a masochist, she craves darker pleasures and gets her wish granted in the form of the Cenobites.

"This is a messy, viscera-soaked, disturbing story that's also lurid and steamy in a way that would make Barker proud. Above all, it's a great addition to the overall mythology, expanding on the briefest glimpse of this Cenobite's human form shown in **Hellraiser II**."

"Sick, but in delicious ways."
—Doug Bradley, **Hellraiser**'s 'Pinhead'

"Barbie Wilde's *Sister Cilice* is devastatingly haunting, piercingly erotic and is one of the true stand-out stories of the anthology."
—<u>All Things Horror</u>

"... a potent piece of nunsploitation. It contains plenty of grotesquerie, and, unlike the majority of the book's other tales, doesn't wait until the end to dish it out!"
—Fright.com

# Reviews for *The Cilicium Trilogy*

"In this impressive collection of short stories, actor Wilde (who played the Female Cenobite in the film classic *Hellbound: Hellraiser II*) reveals a world of beautiful fear. The most delightfully terrifying entries form *The Cilicium Trilogy*, which reveals the complex origin and destiny of Sister Cilice. This character-focused exploration is sensual in its brutality...

"...As much a chilling collection of frightful fiction as a delight for the darker senses, this is a satisfying triumph in a befitting, unforgiving, style.

"Raised from the dead, this phantasmagoria of tales offers well-written mini-nightmares that will traumatize, titillate, and stick in your mind long after you've closed the book. The᾿ Cilice' trilogy imagines the beginnings and further adventures of Wilde's 'Female Cenobite᾿ character. She's given a name, her own agency, and like Julia in the first two *Hellraiser* films, has a vicious streak fed by suffering, pleasure, and power. In fact, Barbie Wilde's imagination rivals Clive Barker himself.
—<u>Fangoria</u>

"I've adored Sister Cilice since she made her first appearance in **Hellbound Hearts** and I'm delighted that Barbie's taken her on a journey through two more installments, completing her arc from sex-hungry nun to one of the major players in Hell; and if you're on the receiving end of her tortures, your suffering will definitely be legendary! She's a Cenobite who gives Pinhead a run for his money, that's for sure.

"In [the second story] Cilice visits the toymaker for her own puzzle-box, the start of her revolution-and in *The Cilicium Rebellion* she shows she's out to show the men how it's really done, along with her elite band of kick-ass female sinners.
"Intoxicating, bloodthirsty and witty, these are stories to make Clive Barker proud. Anyone who loved **The Scarlet Gospels** will be in Heaven, not Hell, reading these..."
—Paul Kane, award-winning and bestselling author/editor of **The Hellraiser Films and Their Legacy**, **Hellbound Hearts** and **Blood RED**

# Reviews for Barbie Wilde's Other Works

"Damaged people, ultraviolence, murder and explicit sex—what's not to love about her work?"

"Wilde is...one of the finest purveyors of erotically charged horror fiction around."
—'Bad Barbie', Featurette by Chris Alexander, Editor-in-Chief, <u>Fangoria</u>

"Seriously, Barbie Wilde's imagination is a place only the brave and twisted should enter."
—<u>Horror After Dark</u>

"...her work is so uncanny and fearless, it is a must have for any horror aficionado." —filmmakers The Soska Sisters (**American Mary, Vendetta, See No Evil 2, Rabid, On The Edge**)

"Barbie Wilde writes like Scheherazade returned from Eblis bearing gorgeously gruesome revelations—like a Cenobite bringing us beauties and horrors from hell."
—award-winning author, Ramsey Campbell

"...perfect and perverse"
—<u>A Girl's Guide to Horror</u>

"Seriously, Barbie Wilde's imagination is a place only the brave and twisted should enter."
—<u>Horror After Dark</u>

"...horrifically bloody, lascivious and wickedly shocking.

"If testosterone jumping erotica combined with heart racing fear is your bag of horror then this is just what you're looking for..."
—Scream Horror Magazine

"The themes of sex and death are inextricably linked, dripping a dark eroticism through many of the stories." "Wilde has a strong voice. In a genre that is often dominated by male authors, she has taken on a leading role."
—Books of Blood

# THE CILICIUM QUADRA

## BY
## BARBIE WILDE

For further information, please visit:

WEB: www.demainpublishing.com
TWITTER: @DemainPubUk
FACEBOOK: Demain Publishing
INSTAGRAM: demainpublishing

# PUBLICATION ATTRIBUTIONS

# ACKNOWLEDGEMENTS

First off, I want to thank Clive Barker for inspiring these stories of mine. His characters and mythology from his original novella, *The Hellbound Heart*, were the basis for the *Hellraiser* film franchise, as well as being the catalyst for these tales of the extraordinary journey of the Female Cenobite, Sister Cilice. The term Renaissance Man is often over-used, but not as far as Clive is concerned. He is an author, artist and poet who has a truly unique vision.

Thanks to award-winning authors, Paul Kane and Marie O'Regan, who asked me to contribute to the *Hellbound Hearts Anthology*, which was based on *The Hellbound Heart*. At that time, I was writing my diary-of-a-serial-killer novel, *The Venus Complex*, and I thought: "Hey, I want to write crime, not horror." But they encouraged to have a go, saying that it would be great to explore the female perspective of the *Hellraiser* mythology. I subsequently wrote *Sister Cilice* in a week. (Something that I've never been able to repeat with any other short story since!)

And thanks to the multi-talented Dean M. Drinkel, who invited me to submit many stories over the years to different horror anthologies and really helped me hone my horror storytelling skills. And many thanks to him for publishing this 'Quadra' of the now four infernal Sister Cilice stories.

Thanks to Chris Alexander, former editor-in-chief of FANGORIA Magazine for his undaunted support for my writing over the years and for interviewing me for his 'Bad Barbie' featurette in FANGORIA #321. He also published the second Sister Cilice story in Gorezone #30.And thanks to Steph Sciullo and Adrian Baldwin for their wonderful artistic contributions to this collection.

To Georg, truly my "ideal reader", who is a never-ending source of inspiration.

# CONTENTS

# SISTER CILICE

*"Loved be pain. Sanctified be pain. Glorified be pain!"*

For many years, Sister Veronica was in the service of a Higher Power. She prayed nine times a day. Her life was work, prayer, a few fitful hours of sleep, then more work, more prayer. Thousands of her pious words floated up to the ether, but no answer was forthcoming; only a cruel, empty silence.

When her depraved dreams became too overwhelming, mortification of the flesh was the only answer. She remembered the Sainted Father Escrivá's maxim on suffering: "Loved be pain. Sanctified be pain. Glorified be pain!" . . . and so she used the whip with greater vengeance, but although she assaulted her flesh, nothing could chase the demons from her mind, those familiars that had tormented her all her life.

\*

Throughout her childhood, entering an Order was the only option available to her—the one way to cleanse her heart of the many sins her parents were convinced she had committed. "Every sin, no matter how inconsequential, is a blemish on your soul and will lead you to eternal damnation," her mother used to say. According to her parents, her every thought, word and deed was sinful. There was no relief from the guilt.

No relief from the remorseless burden of her countless transgressions. And no relief from her rage, which she hid from the world along with her dark fantasies of revenge and pain. Sexual thoughts and acts were forbidden, of course, but that didn't mean these evils left her alone. Perhaps celibacy made it worse, although how was she to know? She'd been sent straight to the Nunnery at the age of seventeen, without even kissing a boy, let alone knowing what it was like to be with a real man in the real world, flesh to flesh. And she would never know.

During her early days in the convent, in an attempt to save her rotten soul, Sister Veronica made the appearance of perfect devotion, to prove to the other Sisters that she had a vocation. Her every act was irreproachable and every word she spoke was blameless. The strain of such unrelenting good behavior, of maintaining such a mask of utter innocence and sanity, was almost unbearable, but her parents—who suffered from an overdose of scrupulosity—had brainwashed her into believing that this was her only way to salvation.

Her predicament got worse when Father Xavier was appointed to celebrate Mass every morning. He was so handsome, so virile, so different from the dried-up, old men that had previously seen to the nuns' spiritual needs. Sister Veronica was convinced that many of the other Sisters felt as she did about him. She could sense their spirits rise when Father Xavier came into the room. Feel the heat from their bodies as they knelt before him as he tenderly ministered the sacraments to them. The occasional accidental touch of Father Xavier's hand on her mouth when he gave her the Host sent little electric shocks through her body. Sister Veronica lived for that random physical contact, even though she knew it was meaningless to him.

Every night, after the others had gone to bed, she would mortify her bare flesh until she bled, but that didn't chase the thoughts of the good Father away, it just made her suffering more sensual. She imagined that Father Xavier was the one with the lash, beating her senseless. She'd fall to the ground exhausted, bleeding, eyes shut, body completely open and vulnerable, imagining his presence standing over her. Still with eyes clenched shut, she would use the leather handle of the whip, pretending it was him—thrusting inside of her, hurting her. His pain was loved, his pain was sanctified, his pain was glorified. She'd stuff a rag in her mouth to stifle her cries. Sister Veronica came for the first time like that: bloody, naked, sweat-soaked, lying on the cold, stone floor. Momentarily sated, yet forever unsatisfied.

After a while, she refined her technique. To heighten her pleasure, she'd take the end of the whip and wrap it around her neck, pushing the handle deep inside her at the same time; each thrust tightening the lash and ever so slightly cutting off the oxygen to her brain to make her orgasms more intense. She would come again and again, shuddering like an old car dieseling on a frosty winter morning. But the taste in her mouth was bitter, because when she opened her eyes, she was alone. Sister Veronica would always be alone. No man would ever come and fill the dry, empty well of her heart. So she would get up, clean herself, wipe away the tears of anger and frustration, kneel on the cold floor and flog herself again and again for her despicable thoughts and acts.

During the day, Sister Veronica would wear a cilice—a small metal chain with inwardly-pointing spikes—around her thigh. She would pull the cilice as tight as she could without cutting off the circulation. It was supposed to remind her of Christ's suffering, but all it did was bring back memories of her private moments with the phantom Father Xavier. Her sexual fantasies were now beginning to torment her during the day. The irony was she could not make penance and cleanse her soul, because the only person she was allowed to confess to was Father Xavier. So the sins just piled up one on top of the other, multiplying and becoming more putrefied with time.

Then a new scenario began to fester in Sister Veronica's mind. She would confess all her sins to Father Xavier. He would be horrified and drag her out of the Confessional to the altar, rip her robes off and scourge her using a whip with metal tips, degrading her flesh until she begged him to stop. Her cast-off blood would stain the fair linen altar cloth and splatter the faces of the Saints' statues. Then Father Xavier would take her, right there on the marble floor in front of the altar, underneath the enormous suspended golden crucifix. His cassock would fall away from him and reveal the wonders of his flawless body and his sex. She could only imagine what it would look like: ivory in color, hard, and shaped like a Knights Templar sword perhaps. In her fantasies, Father Xavier used not only his saintly member to impale her, but any other implement to hand—the holier the better—to sanctify and cleanse her polluted body and diseased mind. Sister Veronica felt her sanity slipping away, fueled by her feverish, obsessive thoughts. Haunted by her desires, she continued to torment her wretched body until it was laced with scars.

Finally, Sister Veronica asked to be assigned to the library archives in the convent's catacomb-like cellar as a way of calming and cooling off her mind. There were thousands of books down there, ancient papers, letters and epistles, missives from Popes and Cardinals. Perhaps she could immerse herself in history to distract herself from her miserably empty present.

It was there, late one night, that Sister Veronica found an ancient manuscript in an old leaden box whose lock had long since rusted away. It was hidden in an alcove far from the entrance, forgotten for centuries. The box was littered with crunchy long-dead black beetles, a few blood-red, dried roses and a dusty mummified crow; beak open and tongue lolling out as if in accusation.

The book was called the *Grimorium Enochia* and it was written in the 15th Century by Raphael Athanasius. Sister Veronica spent weeks trying to translate the Latin text. For the first time in years, something was taking her mind away from the bloody world of her profane imaginings. She soon realized that she had discovered something far more engrossing than her fantasies. Athanasius was an alchemist, necromancer and cryptographer, and had been a friend of the notorious serial killer, dabbler in the black arts, and brother-in-arms to Jeanne d'Arc, Maréchal Gilles de Rais.

At first glance, Athanasius's book appeared to be about his accounts of summoning forth and speaking with angels and demons. However, it soon became obvious to Sister Veronica that his manuscript was far more than just a few incantations and stories. Athanasius's invocations were a pathway into another dimension: a place where the chthonic inhabitants might understand her needs. These beings were called Cenobites and were members of another kind of Order altogether, where pain as pleasure was the norm, not a hidden vice. She was intrigued and hopeful that somehow she might be allowed access into this world, to find an answer to her torment from those who seemed to be fellow travelers.

She knew by now that she was tired of her life, disgusted by it, not because of what she did to herself, not because of her secrets and sins, but because she had always been a slave to other people's demands. She had never been in charge—never allowed to follow her cravings—subject to countless indignities of the spirit. She was soul-sick, but it wasn't her fault. She needed to get out and Athanasius offered her the way. Not back to the real world of pathetic, ordinary people, which she despised because it reminded her of her parents and all those other contemptible, hypocritical sycophants, but moving into a murky, labyrinthine sanctuary of lust, pleasure, pain, power and blood ruled by the un-divine Order of the Gash.

*

After several abortive attempts, Sister Veronica finally deciphered Athanasius's infernal recipe. Of course, the correct procedure was important, but as she delved into the text, Sister Veronica realized that she already possessed the most essential and vital ingredient for success: the overwhelming desire to invoke the Schism that would allow the

Cenobites to enter into this realm and show her their marvels.

She prepared for their entrance with care, finding an abandoned, airless room adjacent to the library where she equipped a makeshift altar with artifacts of torture that she thought would amuse the Cenobites. In the hospital adjacent to the convent, she found a terminally sick child who was too far gone to notice the pint of blood that she furtively collected from him at the fourth hour after midnight. She mixed this with some of her own menstrual blood and poured the mixture into a Chalice that she appropriated from the convent's chapel. She also added her own scourge and cilice as personal decorations to her altar.

As Sister Veronica uttered the final cadence of Athanasius's Latin invocation, she heard the tinkle of chimes, almost too cloying and sweet to her ears, then a mournful bell tolling. The sounds weren't coming from above, but from somewhere near her, down here in the dark catacombs where not long ago, dead bodies of nuns (and as rumor would have it, their illegitimate murdered offspring) were buried. The lights fluttered in time to the bell and she knew that it wasn't just an ordinary power fluctuation. Something, someone, was coming. A twinge of regret stabbed her heart, a touch of panic, but she pushed it away with a mental growl. She was sick to death of fear, tired of being ashamed of nothing, weary of being a weakling. She wanted strength and power and sensation for its own sake. She longed to discipline others, to make them feel as she had. She wanted to be destroyed and remade again.

Another sound entered her mind, the sound of a metronome ticking, ticking, ticking— in time to the quickened beating of her heart. The walls of the room groaned in time to the metronome—they bulged and heaved, and between the cracks of the stones, she saw light—a yellowy, sickly, white light. The walls shuddered and she stumbled back to the doorway, ready to make a hasty retreat if her courage failed her. Finally the walls parted, dust erupted in a brownish, rancid cloud—more light spilled into the room, and voices beautiful, but discordant, warbled in the background, like a movie soundtrack played at the wrong speed.

A tall, male Cenobite entered, followed by a few others, but she had no interest in them. She gasped, not in horror, but in admiration. The Leader was stunning, a fallen angel, his princely beauty still shining through, even though his face and body were mutilated and twisted by scars, lacerations, pins, wires and nails. His black eyes were liquid with eternal suffering; eyelids stapled permanently open. His long, black, leather apron was soaked with blood and speckled with bits of flesh. His naked arms were laced with multiple cilices and the razor-sharp, inward spikes poked deeply into his flesh. Barbed wire was wrapped around his chest and chains bound his legs. He held a black leather and steel-capped cat-o'-nine-tails in his gloved hand and she knew who it was for: a special gift just for her. Sister Veronica sank down to her knees and opened her arms wide in a pretty, Madonnaesque pose of gratitude. He smiled, showing perfect bloodied teeth, filed into flawless little points.

A strong, warm wind scented with vanilla billowed up from behind him, knocking Sister Veronica down to the ground. Her robes fluttered up, exposing her secret places and momentarily blinding her. She lifted her arms above her head, and her clothes and veil ripped off and flew off into the darkness, like an enormous, demented crow.

He stared at Sister Veronica—the naked, surrendered nun—and he was still smiling, almost puzzled by her rapt acceptance. He spoke, his voice echoing in the chamber, "Do you know what you are asking of us? Do you know what will happen to you?"

Sister Veronica answered, "Yes, with all my heart. Take me. Make me one of you, if you think I'm worthy. I'll give anything to you. Soul, body, mind, heart. You know they are already yours, if you want them."

He laughed, joined by the others hidden back in the darkness. His merriment didn't frighten Sister Veronica, it just exhilarated her and made her desperate for his embraces.

She longed to stand up and go to him, but her limbs refused to move. Sister Veronica felt something tightening at her wrists and ankles, looked and saw silvery, spiked chains pulled tight by unseen hands disappearing into the darkness—stretching her limbs out to their fullest extent, as if she was strapped to an invisible torture rack. The pain of the diamond-sharp spikes digging into her skin was excruciating, but it was nothing compared to the new sensations that were flooding her body. It was as if all her nerve endings were on fire, alert to every mote of dust that landed on her exposed flesh, every grain of dirt being ground into her back and buttocks. She felt like she was being burned at the stake; even breathing hurt—the air stung her lungs. But the pain, instead of being maddening or frightening, just sent her deeper into a bizarre ecstasy. Below her waist, the epithelial fire was flickering up her thighs, then darting inside her—burning her internally with wave after wave of searing, orgasmic thrusts.

Sister Veronica screamed and writhed, pleasure and pain mixed in an infernal cocktail. It was what she always dreamed of, but more. The male Cenobite laughed again, enjoying her delicious agony, and began working his personal magic with his scourge over her naked breasts and genitals. How was it possible to feel more pain? How was it possible to feel more pleasure?

In the shadows, the other Cenobites applauded the show. They hadn't seen anything this entertaining in ages.

The metal hooks on the leather strips of his scourge dug into Sister Veronica's skin and gouged out her flesh. She felt that not only her body was being flayed, but her soul. She didn't care, she desperately wanted release from her old self. She was happy to trade that tired bag of flesh for something else, something beautiful—like HIM. She wanted to be him: intractable, indomitable, powerful, a slave to nothing, but desire. She wanted his nails, pins, wires, fingers and teeth to bite into her, to destroy and then transmute her sad sack of sin into a blood-drenched angel of darkness—the envy of all the other demons. She sent this message to him in her shrieks of horrified delight and gratitude.

He finally stopped and dropped his drenched whip. He walked over and stood astride her body. The pain hadn't abated and Sister Veronica still cried out. He sunk down slowly, a knee planted on each side of her chest and took out a thin-bladed surgical scalpel. He leaned over, placed his hand under her chin and gently pushed back her head. Unable to scream, feet pummeling the ground, Sister Veronica made muffled sounds of anguish as he slowly and artistically carved a new orifice for her. He laced thin platinum wires through her cheeks and, using these as an anchor, hooked and pulled the skin away from her gaping wound. When he had finished, he straightened up and lifted his apron to show her another present he had prepared for her.

The skin fire was nothing. Her bloody wound was nothing. The agonizing whips and chains were nothing. Whatever happened to Sister Veronica next would obliterate her forever, tear her apart and send her whirling down into an abyss of divine degradation, to that special place she had longed to go to for so many years.

The Cenobite entered her, using every orifice, old and new. Sister Veronica's choking, dreadful moans of passion gurgled from her lips, but the sounds were triumphant, and her frantically thrashing body echoed her exquisite feelings of the ultimate in sensual suffering.

Her shadowy Cenobite audience applauded yet again. What a girl! The good Sister's adoration for mutilation, sensation and agony would be legendary, even in Hell.

*

For many years now, Sister Cilice has been in the service of a Subterranean Power. Hellbound to glory. She has no thoughts, no worries, no guilt, no empathy, no passion, no dreams, nothing to do but to satiate desires that can never really be quenched to the full, but hell, nothing is perfect. She assists her Leader in his work; they are a perfect team. They even finish each other's threats to those who dare call upon them and take turns flaying those unfortunates who thought they knew what they were doing when they summoned the Order of the Gash. Silence from above no longer greets her words, but screams for mercy from below. They pray to Sister Cilice now. They are her supplicants, not the other way around. The mortification of her flesh no longer gives her quite the pleasure it used to, but the delight in the pain of others is truly enriching. She is no longer concerned about the demons in her mind. She is a demon herself now and woe betide the mind that comes across her.

In a tiny corner of the shriveled, blackened brain that once belonged to someone called Sister Veronica, Sister Cilice hears an echo of one phrase above all others: "Loved be pain. Sanctified be pain. Glorified be pain!"

They are the only words that can still make her laugh.

# THE CILICIUM CONFIGURATION

*"Hell needs a little glamour . . ."*

Sister Cilice was a first level Female Cenobite of the Order of the Gash and she was bored . . . She yearned for a break from the eternity of exquisite, controlled experimentation on those souls whose reckless pursuit of pleasure for its own sake had led them to the Cenobites. She paced her ascetic, lead-lined, monkish cell in the Second Quadrant of the Labyrinth, ignoring the squawking pleas of her pet crow Xibalbá, who constantly begged for his favorite treat of human eyeballs marinated in red wine.

She fancied a little weekend jaunt away from Hell's environs, so Sister Cilice resolved to visit the Toymaker, a legendary creator of intricate puzzle boxes, unique playthings and mechanical birds. And she'd never been to Paris, a fabled city that was considered far too sinful when she was enduring her first incarnation as a desolate, sex-starved nun in a dismal, run-down convent in the Vendée region of Western France.

Sister Cilice was fascinated by the idea that a mere human could somehow construct the glittering, mysterious puzzle boxes that could invoke her hellish cohorts so readily. This was especially intriguing to her, because her method of conjuring up the Schism and becoming one with the Order of the Gash had been so different from the others of her ilk. Sister Cilice's ceremony had involved offerings of blood and roses, a discreet sacrifice of a sick child, and chanting the incantations of the corrupt monk and sorcerer, Raphael Athanasius. (Athanasius had been a *compadre* to the infamously depraved 15th century French general, child serial killer and spendthrift, Gilles de Rais.) Of course, the crowning ingredient in her infernal recipe was . . . desire.

Sister Cilice slipped into the Lead Cenobite's quarters and "borrowed" the Ianua Mechanism, a device of luminous beauty whose platinum and obsidian components were fashioned from the designs of 14th century alchemist extraordinaire, Albertus Magnus, which he in turn had borrowed from the Greek mathematical and engineering genius, Archimedes. It was the only device that could open the rarely used Reverse Schism to enable the Cenobites to freely travel to the dimension of *Homo sapiens*—without the participation of humans themselves. Under the strict rules that governed the use of the Ianua Mechanism, Sister Cilice wasn't allowed to use it for her own purposes, but as it was employed so infrequently, she doubted that the Lead Cenobite would notice it was missing.

Sister Cilice travelled through the time portal—arriving at the Toymaker's eccentric residence in the artisans' quarter of 18th century Paris in an instant. Re-materializing in a corridor outside his workshop located in the basement *cave* underneath his house, Sister Cilice entered the arched doorway to find him kneeling on the stone floor, deeply involved in the process of strangling yet another prostitute. (Prostitutes were easy prey for the Toymaker. He was able to entice them to his house for the price of a loaf of bread, where he killed them and boiled them down to their base components. The fatty deposits under their stomach muscles were an essential constituent for the greasing of the puzzle box's precious gears.)

Sister Cilice intuitively knew that the naked young prostitute's last moments were nigh, as her body was going through some thrillingly spasmodic death throes, so she stopped time for a moment. The Toymaker was frozen, but the girl was in Sister Cilice's cocoon of time and space. She swooped down and clamped her lips over the girl's wide open, imploring mouth. Sister Cilice was delighted by the girl's warm, velvety tongue squirming inside her mouth. She sucked in the girl's last breath—vacuuming up her soul in the bargain. The young prostitute juddered, thrashed her voluptuous, pale thighs against the floor and died.

Sister Cilice stepped back behind the Toymaker and resumed time. She was amused to see him trying to kiss the dead prostitute— no doubt hoping to get a taste of her last honeyed breath himself. When he realized that the wretched whore had already expired, he released his grasp around her neck with such disappointed abandon that her head dropped to the floor with a thud. This caused Sister Cilice to rasp out a desiccated laugh. The Toymaker swung around in surprise and anger, then fell prostrate on the floor with respect and humility, not expecting to see such a distinguished visitor without prior notice. He dared to raise his eyes to drink in her deathly presence: the dead blue-white skin; the bloodstained, black, tight-fitting, leather nun's habit; the silver piercings that lashed through her face; the open wounds that would never heal; and the baleful, emerald-green eyes that looked at him with such scorn.

"Get up, Toymaker, and show me these wonders of yours," Sister Cilice demanded. He leapt to his feet and proudly presented his wares: intricate, beautiful, artistic, musical puzzle boxes that would have astonished her if she was still human. However, even Sister Cilice could admire his handiwork, especially knowing the malevolent secrets and terrors of visceral carnality that the boxes could unleash upon their chosen supplicants.

Then an idea popped into her rebellious mind. It had always annoyed Sister Cilice that she was a *Subordinatus* to the Lead Cenobite. She wanted her own order, her own "scream" of demons. In her midnight plottings, she had already given the New Order a name: "The Sisterhood of the Cilice." The idea of adding more females under her command to populate the vast dungeons of the Underworld was a delicious one. After all, Hell needed a bit of glamour.

"Toymaker, I want you to make a special puzzle box dedicated to me and me alone. A Cilicium Configuration that will attract needy females desiring the ultimate in sensuality—with designs incorporating things of special meaning to me: blood-red roses, a murder of my favorite, vermillion-eyed crows (and how I delight in that particular collective noun) and silver cilices."

The Toymaker was a bit hazy on what a cilice exactly was, so she showed him, lifting her long leather skirt to reveal her legs and vulva entwined with silver chains. The chains were adorned with tiny hooks that stabbed into her bloodstained flesh—the *sanguineus* fluids long dried and blackened. Like the hair shirts of old, cilices were designed to remind the wearer of the suffering of the Savior. Ironic that they had become part and parcel of Sister Cilice's depraved sexual fantasies back in her old life at the convent, before her Rapture—before her transformation into the dark-hearted demonic angel that she now was.

As they discussed the designs, Sister Cilice came up with her *pièce de résistance:* the alchemical symbol for female—

—which was also a representation of the Greek goddess of love, Venus—had to be stamped on each box.

For two weeks, the Toymaker obediently labored over the design and construction of the Cilicium Configuration, while a veiled Sister Cilice explored and enjoyed the seamier elements of Paris during the dead of night.

As instructed, the Toymaker was to test the box before delivery, so he plotted to meet with the beautiful, but notorious Duchess de Mortamour, whose reputation for everything transgressional was chattered about under the breaths of the powerful men and women of the court, but never out in the open. The Duchess's husband, the Duc de Mortamour, was far too influential with the king and no one dared to cross him.

The Duchess was an admirer of the so-called Blood Queen, the Hungarian Countess Elizabeth Báthory de Ecsed, who was reputed to have killed over six hundred women and young girls in the early 17th century so she could bathe in their blood in order to maintain her youthful appearance. The Duchess was also reputed to have dabbled in the dark arts and murdered a few young women herself, but since many of these rumors centered on women that the Duc himself had dallied with, her bloodthirsty streak may have had more to do with jealousy than magic.

The Toymaker made an appointment with the Duchess, promising her an intriguing puzzle box with bold motifs laced with intricate textures. His reputation preceded him and the Duchess was eager to inspect his workshop.

A time was set for her appointment just after midnight. As instructed, she hadn't told anyone of the assignation and arrived veiled and dressed in black via a hired coach and four.

The Toymaker escorted her to his workshop and the Duchess was suitably impressed with not only the array of puzzle boxes laid before her, but also the lifelike mechanical birds that tweeted melodiously in the background. He took the Duchess to a small private room in the back, where the Cilicium Configuration was displayed on a table dressed as an altar next to some dried red roses and a decanter full of unspecified red liquid.

"Behold, my masterpiece, designed for your pleasure!" the Toymaker proclaimed with a wave of his hand. The Duchess moved forward to examine the box and he withdrew from the room discreetly. He entered a nearby closet and removed a small portrait from the wall. Secreted behind the portrait was a peephole, where he could spy on the proceedings in the private room.

The Duchess picked up the puzzle box, admiring its silver, ebony and ruby encrusted designs. Her hands flew over the surface— moving the beautifully engineered segments as if she had designed it herself, then she stopped suddenly and put down the puzzle box, as she was overcome with an almost stultifying wave of heat and nausea. Sweat broke out on her brow and her silken clothes, so comfortable before, became scratchy and burdensome— almost burning her skin. She tore at the buttons at her throat, trying to remember how the dress came off, because she was so used to maids dressing and undressing her.

In desperation, the Duchess resorted to frantically rending the dress from her body, finally collapsing in a naked heap on the floor. It was then that she heard the discordant but compelling, tinkling melody of the Cilicium Configuration calling to her. She dragged herself up the altar, exhausted and burning with an internal fire. She swept the roses and decanter off the altar and lay down on her back—the puzzle box in her hands, fingers fiddling with the moving panels, feverishly desiring an answer, craving an escape from her boring life at court, yearning for a sensuality beyond anything offered here on earth. The device felt her wet, pulsating fingers and heard her panting desires and the panels began to move by their own accord, fashioning themselves into a different kind of mechanism—one designed to give pleasure to solitary women.

The Duchess was thrilled at this new love toy and placed the Cilicium Configuration between her legs. She slowly inserted it inside her vagina, which was more than ready to embrace the device's vibrating pleasures. At first, the experience was almost overwhelming—more than any man had given her over her years of debauchery. The Duchess shuddered and orgasmed, screaming her release.

Then the noises from the Cilicium Configuration changed tune. Its vibrations became more urgent and the Duchess became frightened. She tried to pull it out, but felt excruciating pain as tiny hooks sprang from the device and fastened themselves to her vaginal wall. She let go and the pain ceased, but the vibrations became more violent and she came again, fearfully, helplessly. For hours it seemed, she suffered the most exquisite, carnal sensations until she was nearly foaming at the mouth.

Finally, it stopped its infernal pulsations. She cautiously pulled it out, gazing with wonder and exhaustion at the bloodstained device. That's when she realized that she was no longer alone.

Sister Cilice stood in a dark corner of the room, smiling at her. She had witnessed the whole ritual and she was pleased beyond measure. Here was a woman whose capacity for sensational sexual suffering neared her own. A perfect addition to the Labyrinth.

"Who are you, wretched woman?" the Duchess demanded. Sister Cilice smiled her wolfish smile again and said, "You called me, I came. Put the Cilicium Configuration back where it was and I will show you such pleasures beyond anything you have experienced before."

"I think I've had enough," the Duchess declared, attempting to get up, but she was frozen on her back, holding the device above her like a dagger. And then it transformed into something else. And the Duchess screamed, but this time it wasn't in pleasure.

*

Sister Cilice was delighted with the Cilicium Configuration and rewarded the Toymaker well with five prostitutes that she had found huddling under a bridge during her brief exploration of Paris. She took the damned and mutilated Duchess back with her to the Labyrinth, transforming her into an acolyte of the Sisterhood of the Cilice.

The Toymaker went back to murdering prostitutes and creating more puzzle boxes, never realizing that he may have played an important part in what became known later in hellish circles as The Cicilium Rebellion of the Female Cenobites.

# THE CILICIUM REBELLION

*"Mother of all demons . . ."*

The air reeked with the dying breaths of corruption. No smothering of the obscene birthday cake-like perfumes of vanilla and cinnamon could obscure the overwhelming stench of the grave that permeated the already fetid gases of the Labyrinth. The prevailing odor was of canned beetroot, one of the few smells that Sister Cilice recalled with particular horror from her previous life as a human, shuddering at the memory of shouted threats at the dinner table unless she finished her plate. Then Sister Cilice laughed . . . the mirthless laughter of the dead. With so much destruction laid before her, her delicate shivers at the thought of the repulsive *Beta vulgaris* were ironic, to say the least.

For the congealed lakes and rivers of Hell were stained black-red with the blood of the Cenobites who refused to bow to her will, along with the Females who had supported her. The cypress trees that lined the highways and byways were bent double by the obsidian winds of change. Crows and ravens flew up squawking to the glowering metallic sky, swirling patterns of revolution and hate and triumph. She had won, but at what cost? She was now the one in power, but dominion over what? Who was left for her to lead? Even her elite team of Female Cenobites had been melded into the atoms of another being more powerful than they could ever have imagined. The devastation was total. There was a tinge of sadness to see the old regime overthrown, but to have been the cause of such total annihilation of her kind was, in a strange way, oddly satisfying.

*

When Sister Cilice was alive in her previous existence, it felt like her mind was drowning in a sea of spiders. Thoughts always racing, scuttling here and there, picking over things, dissecting her digressions, her transgressions. She had longed for freedom from the hideous monotony of her life. The emptiness inside her could not be filled. All she longed for was release.

When her transformation came, as it came to all those who called the Order of the Gash, it tore her apart and put her back together again into a new form: strong and beautiful; ripped and cruel. Sister Cilice was no longer the pathetic human that everyone, including herself, despised, but something else: better, brighter, more purposeful. Someone who was in control.

This took a long time to achieve, of course. No one is invited to the top table in a day. Decades went past before she was accepted as one of the elite. Her mind, her earlier life (if you could call it that), was just a burned-out remnant, but there was still a whisper of a personality in there, someone who took joy in her work. She wasn't just an underling who slavishly took orders from her betters. After all, that's what she'd escaped from back in her old life, her alive but dead life. Now that she was dead, but oh-so-alive, she was aware of so many possibilities.

She was mostly left on her own to pick and choose those who sought them out. It was rare when a human needed the attention of more than one of her kind. She sent out her thoughts, like the delicate tendrils of a spider's web—any little quiver on the line and she would concentrate her attention on the prey. They were so questing and curious, these mortals. Not content with a roof over their heads, food, sex and money. They longed for power too, and sensation, and other things that being comfortable and happy wouldn't allow them to possess. They were the discontented ones, the travelers, the explorers, the ones who lived in-between the cracks of normal society.

After the creation of her own secret Cilicium Configuration—one that would only metamorphose Female Cenobites—Sister Cilice slowly accrued like-minded creatures who would happily follow her to the depths of desire and sensuality. But she wanted something more. Something more meaningful than what she had achieved already. She wanted total dominion.

She walked up and down her lead-lined ascetic cell in the deepest confines of the Labyrinth, conveniently located next to a viscous black lake of blood and guilt. (Uncannily, especially since his *Inferno* was a work of fiction, Dante got the 9th Circle of Hell absolutely right.) Although outwardly cool and tranquil, Sister Cilice's mind raged with a white heat, generated by years of poisonous emotions that had fueled a thousand wars up in the human world: anger, jealousy and humiliation. Strange to think that she had hit the proverbial glass ceiling down in Hell, but that's exactly what had happened. The Lead Cenobite prevented any further advancement for Females in Hell. Why? Just because he could. Because it pleased him to annoy his colleagues. Because he was the one who wanted all the power. He enjoyed putting obstacles in the way of the desires of Sister Cilice, who was more ambitious than the rest of the Females.

So she plotted and paced her narrow room, dreaming of revenge and rebellion, accompanied by the raucous caws of her pet crow, Xibalbá.

*

Finally, to fulfill her dreams of domination, Sister Cilice devised a simple plan: who, what, where, when.

Who? A carefully picked team of the most lethal Females that she could find in the Labyrinth.

What? To conceive of a rebellion that would shake the foundations of Hell and usurp the Lead Cenobite who presently ruled.

Where and When? Sister Cilice planned an assault during the next Grand Conference of Cenobites at Plato's Retreat—sardonically named after the infamous 1980s nightclub in the ultimate of sin cities, New York.

The first thing to do was pick her team. To Sister Cilice, there could be only four other inhabitants of Hell that would fit the bill to be co-leaders of her small but well-trained Female Cenobite army: Lilith, Eve, Cleopatra the Alchemist and Jeanne d'Arc.

Lilith, the first wife of Adam and an eternal seductress and child murderer, was experienced, clever and voracious. Having been booted out of the Garden of Eden for being an independent soul, she still had a considerable chip on her winged shoulder.

Eve, still smarting for being blamed for Original Sin, had been bubbling with rage and passion for millennia. If these emotions could be harnessed, she would be a ferocious opponent.

Cleopatra the Alchemist was no relation to the well-known historic Queen of Egypt. No, this Cleopatra had lived the 3rd Century AD and she was one of the few alchemists who truly possessed the knowledge of creating the Philosopher's Stone—turning base metals into gold or silver for her grateful clients. A magician and scientist of the highest order, Cleopatra would be of great assistance to the rebellion.

And finally, the not-so-saintly Jeanne d'Arc, who used her experience leading the armies of the French in 1429 to become a fine military tactician in the Labyrinth. Before being burned at the stake, Jeanne was unfortunately influenced by her emotionally debauched compatriot, Maréchal de France Gilles de Rais. She rather smudged her image as a devout farm girl by taking part in some rituals devised to bring forth demons to assist the French in their battle to expel the English from their lands. So being burned as a witch was actually not so unjust as it appeared.

*

It was in one of their group Female Cenobite preparatory meetings that Cleopatra had a brainstorm. Why not tinker with the Cilicium

Configuration and twist its function from the creation of Female Cenobites into something far more diabolical: draining the power and strength from the targeted Male Cenobites? It would be so much more satisfying to leave them helpless, than to simply destroy them. Especially since the Lead Cenobite had the annoying habit of reconstituting himself even after his countless and inexplicable obliterations over the years.

Cleopatra took the Cilicium Configuration to her laboratory, where she worked for days carefully experimenting on its internal mechanisms: moving levers and adjusting tempos and balances, as well as altering its all-important melody. The music of the puzzle box was vital to its function, as the tinkling and sinuous notes would not only trigger the gateways of Hell to open and allow access to other dimensions, but also to funnel the Labyrinthine energy needed to torment and transform the chosen ones.

The leaders of the Rebellion met in Sister Cilice's cell when Cleopatra was ready to present her revamped version of the Cilicium Configuration. Its inner workings had been modified to accommodate its new purpose: the subjugation of the Male Cenobites and the castration of their powers.

Sister Cilice was thrilled with the new device, although caution weighed on her mind. Females were outnumbered in Hell, for the simple reason that women just weren't as deadly or dissolute as men. If they were to attack, it had to be a devastating first assault. She'd learned from her readings of Italian philosopher Machiavelli that one had to utterly destroy one's enemies in the first instance, so they couldn't regroup and come back to wreak a terrible revenge on their tormentors.

Although Cleopatra had theoretically tested the Cilicium Configuration in her laboratory, she recommended that they should try the device out practically, but where and on whom? Eve suggested that they use the neglected basement of Plato's Retreat. Fortunately, she still possessed the keys to the place from her younger, wilder days as a topless waitress and burlesque artist there. The Five Females agreed to meet on Monday night (when Plato's was closed) at the stroke of 4 a.m.—that special time beloved of demons when they were at their most powerful and where they could easily enter the minds of humans and cause chaos.

The second problem was who to choose as their guinea pig. Lilith proposed a Male Cenobite who had been pursuing her for decades. She often had dreams of destroying him, because he was so annoying and pathetic in his adoration of her, so he would be easy prey.

The Five Females split up and amused themselves until the appointed day and hour, when they arrived at Plato's Retreat. They entered the deserted baroque style nightclub by the back entrance, moving silently and directly to the door of the basement.

Descending the stairs, Jeanne directed the other Females to fan out and hide, leaving Lilith in the center of the room, lit by a single flickering bare light bulb.

And so they waited . . .

At 4:30 a.m., they heard the clumping sounds of the Male Cenobite arriving for his amorous tryst. Lilith's bird feet scrabbled on the stone floor, eagerly anticipating the glorious end to her cloying admirer.

The Male entered. His name was Malachi and his main job was as an overweight leather-clad messenger boy and acolyte to the Lead Cenobite. His tongue was almost hanging out in desire, very unseemly for one of their kind, and all the Females were eager to see what the Cilicium Configuration had in store for him.

Lilith couldn't resist a bit of seduction, so without a word she walked up to Malachi and hungrily kissed him on his ruined and disfigured lips. He responded enthusiastically and she forced him down to his knees. He buried his head in her muscular thighs. That's when Sister

Cilice gave Lilith a sign. Lilith grabbed Malachi's thinning hair, pulled his head back and viciously slashed Malachi across the face with a hidden dagger, slicing his eyeballs in half. He shrieked and covered his face with pierced and tattooed hands.

Lilith slipped back into the shadows and Sister Cilice moved into position with the Cilicium Configuration. This was the moment they'd all been waiting for. She followed Cleopatra's instructions to the letter, setting the Configuration into motion and placing it on the floor between the blinded Male Cenobite's knees.

The puzzle box danced and sighed its charmingly discordant tunes. Malachi was too distracted with pain to notice. Then the top of the puzzle box sprung open and thin chains of silvery platinum shot out from its darkly intricate interior, the hooks at the ends of the chains embedding themselves into Malachi's leather clad genitalia. Blood seeped out and trickled down the chains into the depths of the

Cilicium Configuration, awakening what lay inside. Malachi shrieked again and tried to pull the hooks out, but that only caused him more pain and, perversely, more pleasure.

Then something else issued forth from the puzzle box. A light blinked on, a twirling blinding light. Too late, the Five Females realized that the Schism had opened up and released a diminutive creature that could not have come from the humans' Earth, but from some other dimension not known to them. The creature popped out from the Cilicium Configuration like a cosmic jack-in-the-box, which it faintly resembled, but the demonic Punch lookalike didn't stay there for long. Abseiling up the silver chains, the creature attached itself and then violently hugged Malachi's blood-soaked crotch.

A diabolical hug, as it turned out. Malachi's moans of pleasure and pain gurgled to a halt. He fell back supine on the ground, legs akimbo, and as the thing squeezed harder, Malachi's body rapidly softened and liquefied like a leather-clad snowman on a hot summer's day. His mouth slacked open and his tongue oozed out, shrinking into an oily slug-like apparition on his face. The creature grew alarmingly in size as it became more engorged with Malachi's personality, power, blood and desiccated organs, while Malachi dissolved into a greasy sludge.

The Females were stunned to say the least. All they were expecting was an entertaining and gruesome castration, not a demonic blood-sucking puppet. Although it was hardly puppet-sized anymore. They should have fled the scene for their own protection, but the Females were too fascinated by the sight to budge from their hiding places.

The creature finished slurping up the remaining Cenobite slime on the floor, then stood and turned around to face them. Its visage had changed, looking less like Punch and more like a mix of the hapless Malachi and a squashed face of a boxer dog. It was human-like in its body shape and the color of its skin was as silvery and metallic looking as the chains that originally sprung from the puzzle box to ensnare Malachi's privates.

Sister Cilice hissed to Cleopatra: "Cleo, what have you done? This thing could destroy us all!"

Cleopatra replied: "All I did was create a device to castrate the males. What this creature is, or where it's from, I have no idea."

Lilith decided that she wanted a closer look at the newcomer and came forward to reveal herself in the light as the ferocious she-demon that she was: winged, buxom and blood-thirsty. Lilith thundered: "Who are you and what do you want?"

The silvery creature sniggered and said: "Lilith, Queen of the Demons, I salute you for your audacity. My name is Mastema. I am the Angel of All Disasters, a punisher of those who offend the powers that be and a flatterer of the first order. You are truly the most splendid of all the lady demons here . . . But you, Sister Cilice, you are of such great beauty that my breath is taken away. Of course, Eve and Jeanne are beyond such measly words as beauty."

Without hesitation, Jeanne unsheathed her sword and attacked Mastema. She screamed in warning to the others: "He is the father of all evil. I recognize his name from the old books!"

Her sword thrust through Mastema's silvery skin like it was butter. The creature looked down in surprise and disappointment at the weapon lodged in his belly and then laughed merrily.

"I see that I shall have to make another demonstration of my power."

Mastema removed Jeanne's sword, leapt forward and embraced her with such strength that she had no time to cry out. He entwined himself around her like a lover and she melted into his arms and diminished with each second until her armor fell to the ground, empty.

Now Mastema's face was an obscene mash-up of Malachi, Jeanne and the boxer dog and he had grown to twice his previous size. Sister Cilice was contemplating a speedy retreat, when the creature spoke.

"Jeanne wasn't really one of you, was she? Rather ineffectual while she was alive, never really achieved anything of note down here. I think that I've done you a favor. Your group is all the stronger for the pruning of its weakest member."

Eve stepped forward: "So what do you offer us then?"

Mastema said: "Dominion. Isn't that what you all want? No more kowtowing to the big boys? I really admire your plan and I'm more than willing to help."

"Why should we trust you?" Lilith snarled.

Mastema giggled and said: "You can't. Isn't that delicious?"

"What is your plan?" Sister Cilice asked.

Mastema beamed with delight: "How does total and utter destruction suit you?"

So the Females made their infernal pact with Mastema, not realizing that he had a hidden agenda of his own. At first, all went well. Sister Cilice gave Mastema one of the Lead Cenobite's leather gauntlets (a trophy from one of their rare moments of mutual sensuality) and Mastema snuffled up the Lead Cenobite's scent and demonic DNA in an instant.

Mastema scampered off like an eager bloodhound, seeking out the Lead Cenobite, taking him unawares in his quarters and enveloping him in one of his terminal embraces. However, the Lead Cenobite was no pushover and fought viciously against Mastema, ripping his left arm off in the struggle. Salamander-like, Mastema's arm grew right back and the brutal battle continued. In the end—his strength sapped by Mastema's relentless attack—the weakened Lead Cenobite collapsed and Mastema absorbed every cynical particle of his being.

The other Male Cenobites got wind of the interloper and a gruesome bloody war of the sexes ensued. Cilicium Configurations were thrown like a whole new dimension of fragmentation grenades. Chains and hooks flew through the air, cutting into and ripping the flesh of both Males and Females alike.

Cleopatra was the first to perish, shredded into tiny pieces by the very puzzle boxes that so fascinated her. The ground was slimed with the gushing, steaming Cenobite gore and Eve slipped and fell—to be decapitated in an instant by a blood-crazed Male wielding an ancient Viking battle ax. Lilith held out the longest, but she eventually expired with feathered wings plucked and burned, and eyes gouged out, ironically echoing her punishment of Malachi's adoration. Even though the Sisterhood was defeated, Sister Cilice fought on, taking no prisoners, slashing and skewering her opponents like a diabolical feminine version of Vlad the Impaler.

In the midst of it all, Mastema fought like a deranged gargantuan ninja warrior, although instead of a samurai sword, his weapon was the fatal touch of his arms and hands, which withered and soaked up Cenobites whenever he came into contact with them.

*

So, instead of the glorious enslavement of the Males, all was blackness, annihilation and the death of the already dead. The only two left standing were Mastema—now enormous, bloated and decorated with the faces of countless Cenobites, with the abiding boxer dog face still the strongest image—and a battle-weary Sister Cilice, surrounded by her murder of crows and ravens.

She realized now that she had been tricked by Mastema. The Labyrinth was an empty smoldering wreck and she was to blame. She wondered why she had been spared Mastema's lethal embraces.

As Sister Cilice surveyed the smoking ruins of Hell, she felt a presence behind her. Her time had come. Well, she would greet oblivion with grace. It was the least she could do.

She turned and looked up. Mastema towered over her, his gluttonous belly swollen with the essences of thousands of her fellow Cenobites. He looked at her fondly, which she found rather disgusting.

"I have always admired you, Sister Cilice," Mastema said. "Your adoration of suffering and torture was second to none and your wonderful back story of being a former nun and willingly giving up your humanity to become a Cenobite always intrigued me. Of course, we knew about your little plot from the beginning, which is why I was inserted into the Cilicium Configuration as the Toymaker was creating it for you all those centuries ago. Malachi's blood and XY chromosomes awakened me and I knew that the game was afoot. Well, what do you think of your Rebellion of the Female Cenobites now?"

"You have destroyed us. I have dominion over nothing. Do what you must and let me follow my fellow Cenobites into the void."

"Oh, my dear, you give up so easily! I was expecting some kind of thrilling, violent, final gesture that would go into the annals of Hell, at the very least."

"Please, just get on with it," she growled.

"You don't understand. I have no intention of destroying you. I love you with all my heart, but sadly, I cannot caress your beautiful, blue and scarified corpse flesh. I can only yearn for your touch from afar like a pimply adolescent schoolboy."

"So you leave me here alone in Hell, destined for an existence of solitude forever?"

"Oh, no, I have plans for you. I have left you a little gift. It's contained within your exquisite Cilicium Configuration. Here it is. Take it back. It was always yours." He offered her the puzzle box, dropping it into her outstretched hand.

"There are many surprises inside. All you have to do is solve the puzzle and you will experience the ultimate in sensual suffering—

what you always offered your victims. Although it's more like sensuality and then suffering."

"What kind of gift lies inside?" asked Sister Cilice.

The creature's laughter was filled to the brim with the screaming cacophony of dead Cenobites, a deeply unpleasant sound. "My sperm! Yes, you can repopulate Hell all on your own. You will be the Mother of All Demons. Think of it: you will no longer be a mere factotum, you will be Queen of the Labyrinth. When you insert the device, millions of demonic seeds will flow and infest your withered womb. I promise that the sensations will be legendary.

"And the suffering?"

Mastema laughed again. "As I just said, you will be the mother of legions of new demons. If the Curse of Eve and the pain of childbirth doesn't kill you, it will make you so strong that you will reign here for eternity. It's your choice: solitude—or the temporary servitude of motherhood, followed by complete domination."

"And you . . . ?"

"Oh, I will change. I will surround you and our children, guard you and protect you. Do you accept the covenant?"

Sister Cilice did not hesitate: "Yes . . ."

"Excellent! Remember that I will always be here with you—albeit in another form. Farewell, sweet Cenobite!"

Mastema turned away, gently rising up like a giant gothic balloon— serenely drifting across the blighted landscape. As Sister Cilice watched, his bulk gradually deflated and spread out like a flying carpet, which then began to spin faster and faster. Eventually, Mastema's whirling body shattered into millions of scintillating snowflakes, which eventually drifted down and covered the blasted ground like a silvery shroud.

Sister Cilice crunched over the icy shards of Mastema's last physical remains. The fires of Hell were quenched and the scenery was beautiful: a new frosty platinum world, an ice cave of wonders—all repainted in her favorite Cilicium Configuration colors of silver, black and red, since the rivers still flowed with the cornelian-colored blood of the expired Cenobites.

Sister Cilice smiled. It hadn't been a tough choice. She played with the puzzle box, sliding her cold fingers over the surface. In the distance, a lonely bell tolled and the conflicted harmonies of the Cilicium Configuration's melodies started to play deep inside the confines of the box. Then the Configuration started to change . . . and Hell began all over again.

# QUEEN OF THE LABYRINTH

*"Dark angels of pain . . ."*

Hell is empty and all the devils are in Cilice's womb. Cenobites, male and female, had been destroyed. Cilice's plan of domination over the males had been shattered by the machinations of a new kind of demon that she didn't even know existed, who had been concealed inside a puzzle box of her own design.

The fires and revolutions of Hell were long since quenched and an empty, frozen, white, red and black landscape stretched into the far distance. Dimensions had been punctured and spectral beings had invaded not only Cilice's infernal kingdom, but the earthy plane as well.

Chaos reigned for a brief time. As she took cover from the storm of angry ravens, distraught minions and discombobulated minor demons, Cilice's eagerly swirling and burbling brood begged to be purged from the constraints of her painfully swollen belly.

Her name was now Cilice, Queen of the Labyrinth. Queen of Nothing. Queen of Pain. There were no ladies-in-waiting to tend to her and when the time came, she would have to give birth to an army of demons on her own, hoping that the swarms of tiny malevolents would not turn on her and rip her to shreds as soon as they were ejected unceremoniously from her uterus with as much love and care as a female crocodile would lavish on her own hatchlings. Or perhaps they would consume her as baby spiders do their mother, once they had issued forth from their arachnid mother's carefully protected egg sac.

So many wonderfully heartless parallels to the world of nature on that distant earthy plane, but here in Hell, she could only fruitlessly speculate on her fate.

*

Mastema, the father of all her demons, had

warned her that when the time came she would be either destroyed or reign triumphant—if she was strong enough. Cilice was confident that she would be. After all, it was her plotting and deviousness that had destroyed Hell in the first place and she was the only one left standing. The least that the Fates could do was let her see Hell re-populated with her own offspring.

As she waited for the time of parturition to come, she constantly reviewed the choice she made: either to reign in Hell for millennia over a new breed of demon of Cilice's and Mastema's cruel design, or to live in solitude for thousands of years. Obviously, unlimited power, even with the threat of death behind it, appealed to her far more than a lonely life as a Cenobitical spinster.

*

So she took the newly transformed box that Mastema had concocted and bestowed upon her—knowingly playing with the smooth sliding surfaces. As soon as she had reached the optimum configuration, she had watched in amazement (or with as much amazement as someone with no feelings could muster) as the box morphed yet again into something else: instead of her design of an infernal dildo that could transform women into Cenobites, the box became a long, octagonal Codex: a device originally invented by Leonardo DaVinci to hold secret messages. However, this one was full to the brim with the demonic sperm of Mastema.

The Codex was also a message in a bottle to future generations. All laments. All configurations. All the miseries that were to beset mankind that had fled from Pandora's magical box, all the chains and hooks and desires and horrors were now going to be manifest in her.

Cilice slowly inserted the codex into her vagina. It was almost too big and the edges painfully slid and scraped along the delicate and fleshy membranes of her most secret place. The pain was delicious. She expertly used the codex to give her pleasure and for the first time in decades, Cilice came, crying out in ecstasy and agony.

The codex seemed to sense her supreme moment of pleasure; a cue for it to release its secret. Mastema's sperm shot out in a thrillingly scalding and seemingly never-ending spurt. She could almost sense the life and the passion that each and every one of his seed possessed. All the thoughts and fantasies of each spermatozoa swarmed into her mind and the sensory overload nearly drove her mad. She screamed her release and her fear until her throat was raw. Would this experience kill her, or make her invincible?

*

When her time came, it was an obscene parody of human childbirth. She crawled and writhed along the ground—regurgitating black, shiny, beetle-sized demons from every orifice: vaginal, anal, nasal, esophageal. The tiniest of Cenobites even managed to squeeze their way through her tear ducts, so she was literally weeping demons. To say that the experience was agonizing was an understatement, but

Cilice endured, as all women have endured the curse of Eve throughout the millennia. Of course, it helped that the sweet suffering she experienced was also pleasurable in a supremely twisted way.

Her infernal babies scuttled and squirmed along the ground—growing fearsomely as they moved. She wondered how they would greet her, how she would control them, if indeed they could be controlled.

She closed her eyes for a brief moment. When she opened them, her demon brood had encircled her, staring at her with the iridescent eyes of insects, dispassionately, eyeing her up to ascertain if she was a threat. One tiny demon squirmed forward and tentatively reached out a minuscule finger to touch her hand. Cilice marveled that even as she looked, the creature was growing.

The finger that had reached out turned into a black pointed hook and stabbed into her hand. Cilice snatched it back, waving her arm furiously and throwing the creature into the distance. She turned and gazed at her brood. They looked up at her with what she could only perceive as hunger in their eyes. She remembered Mastema saying that they would either kill her, or make her stronger.

Cilice made a break for it. She turned and leapt up into the air, jumping over her brood. She landed and ran for the cavern mouth that led down to the barren cells of the Cenobites. She looked briefly behind her and saw that the glittering humming swarm of demon babies was chasing her, like earthbound bees. She ran as fast as she could—leaping over the dead smoldering bodies of Cenobites, past the mayhem, past the screaming crows, past the icy blue and red rivers flowing with cenobitical blood. Into the long dark corridors of hell....

*

Entering the mouth of the cavern, she continued to navigate the narrow corridors. At one point she paused: to the left was a wider hallway that led to the great auditorium where in more civilized times, the Cenobites met and discussed the future of pain and pleasure. She began to move down to the left, thought better of it and went down the darker, narrower passageway to the right. It inclined steeply and she wasn't sure where it led, but at this point, she was past caring.

She was brought up short by a massive iron door barring her way. She glanced behind her, but didn't hear the ominous humming of her brood. She grabbed the handle of the door and to her relief, it opened easily.

She went through and shut the door behind her. There was a bar handy and she was able to secure the door.

She continued down to the bowels of hell, passing empty cellars full of wooden and glass cabinets. She didn't have time to explore them, but they were full of bizarre exhibits, instruments of exquisite torture and objects of terror and beauty.

She finally came to the end of the corridor, which spread out into a vast room. There was a chair in the middle of the room and someone was sitting in it.

Cilice was astounded. She had thought that all the Cenobites had been consumed by the dreadful embraces of death that Mastema had engineered to absorb the essences of all the Cenobites.

The person sat very still... as if waiting for this moment to arrive.

Cilice moved closer cautiously... the figure was too far away for her to recognize who it was.

It didn't move. It didn't react to her presence. It just sat there with infinite patience.

She finally got close enough to see who it was. It was very fitting indeed that the only survivor of the mass destruction in the Labyrinth was one of the most infernal, inspirational figures of history and a long time resident of this timeless, hellish dimension. The man who put the "S" in "S&M" himself.

The "patron saint" of Cenobites, notorious libertine and author of such scandalous tomes as *Justine* and *The 120 Days of Sodom*, Donatien Alphonse François (AKA the Marquis De Sade), smiled as she walked up to him. He looked like a corrupt version of Einstein, with wild white hair, cruel lips, twinkling eyes and a knowing intelligence.

"Hello, my dear!" De Sade said cheerfully, as he had been waiting for her for centuries. "Welcome to my dominion. I have noted with interest your capacity for delicious destruction and bottomless desire, along with the requisite pleasure and pain, of course. *Time to frolic*, my darling Cenobite!"

Sister Cilice smiled her deadly smile. Finally, a creature that was truly her dreamboat of a partner had manifested himself. They would both be legends in Hell. Dark angels of pain . . .

# BIOGRAPHY

Barbie Wilde is best known for playing the Female Cenobite in Clive Barker's classic British cult horror movie, *Hellbound: Hellraiser II*. Before moving to the UK, Wilde attended Syracuse University in the United States, majoring in Drama and Anthropology. She continued her education in London, studying Drama, Classical Mime and Art History, before joining Britain's largest classical mime troupe, SILENTS.

Wilde also was a vicious thug in Michael Winner's *Death Wish 3*; robotically danced in the Bollywood blockbuster, *Janbazz*; and played a drummer in an electronica band in *Grizzly II: The Concert* (finally completed after 37 years and released in 2020 as *Grizzly 2: Revenge*), which starred then unknowns George Clooney, Laura Dern and Charlie Sheen. She featured in 16 TV different shows in the 1980s and 1990s, such as *The Morecambe and Wise Show*,

*Rebellious Jukebox, Pukaski: The TV Detective* and *Hale and Pace*.

In the early 1980s, Wilde sang and danced professionally at the top nightclubs and rock venues of New York, London, Bangkok and Amsterdam with her music and dance group, SHOCK. SHOCK released 2 singles on RCA Records and supported Gary Numan, Ultravox, Depeche Mode and Adam & the Ants.

Wilde also featured in 14 pop videos for various artists such as Ultravox and Simple Minds. Wilde wrote and presented 7 music and film review TV programs in the 1980s and 1990s, interviewing such artists such as Iggy Pop, The Sisters of Mercy, Black, Wet Wet Wet, The B-52s, Johnny Rotten and Cliff Richard, as well as actors Nicolas Cage and Hugh Grant.

In 2009-2021, Wilde contributed short stories to 16 different horror or crime anthologies and publications. Her 2009 Hellraiser-inspired short story, 'Sister Cilice', made it to the top of the list of Dread Central's 8 Most Gruesome

Hellraiser Stories Told Outside the Movies: "This is a messy, viscera-soaked, disturbing story that's also lurid and steamy in a way that would make Barker proud."

In 2012, Comet Press published Wilde's debut diary-of-a-serial killer novel, *The Venus Complex*, prompting America's best-selling horror magazine Fangoria to call her, "one of the finest purveyors of erotically charged horror fiction around". *The Venus Complex* was released as an audio book in autumn 2018, narrated by the "King of Pain" himself, Hellraiser's Doug Bradley.

Wilde's illustrated collection of short horror stories, *Voices of the Damned*, published by SST Publications in 2015, was called, "sensual in its brutality" and "a delight for the darker senses" in a starred review from *Publishers Weekly*. Each of the 11 stories is introduced by a full color artwork and-or illustration created by some of the most imaginative artists in the genre: Clive Barker, Nick Percival, Steve

McGinnis, Daniele Serra, Eric Gross, Tara Bush, Vincent Sammy and Ben Baldwin. *Voices of the Damned* was nominated for the Best Horror Story Collection Award by This is Horror, 2015.

Wilde's most recent short story is 'Liaison' (theme: Lust), which features in the horror anthology, *Circles of Hell*, inspired by Dante's Inferno and published by TK Pulp.

Wilde is collaborating as co-producer and co-screenplay writer with ex-Fangoria Editor-in-Chief and director Chris Alexander (*Blood for Irina*, Parasite Lady, etc.) on the feature length horror movie, *Blue Eyes.*

Wilde returned to acting in the Amazon Prime horror series Dark Ditties Presents... in the episodes *The Offer* (2017) and *Dad* (2022), as well as playing a high society cannibal queen in *Body Horror: Eating Disorders* (2024).

Barbie Wilde is the proud recipient of the Texas Frightmare Weekend Lifetime of Torment

Award 2018 and the Cine-Excess Innovator of Horror Award 2023.

# STEPH SCIULLO – ART

Steph Sciullo's work has been called grotesque, dark, disturbing and visceral. She is a self-taught visual artist from Pittsburgh and works across a wide variety of mediums including sculpting, painting, drawing, printmaking and assemblage. Steph uses a variety of materials in her work including wax, wood, clay, acrylics, inks, stains, and found objects.

Steph shows in various galleries and sells work not only online, but at various curiosity shops and horror conventions throughout the country.

"Steph's work is challenging and highly original: grotesque, beautiful, twisted, funny, demented and downright fucked-up!"
—Doug "Pinhead" Bradley

"I'd buy her whole collection if I could!"
—Sid 'Captain Spaulding' Haig

"Stunning, sensual, unique, controversial, gore-geous: what's not to love about Steph's work?" —Barbie Wilde, Author (*The Venus Complex*, *Voices of the Damned*, *Sister Cilice*) and Actress (Female Cenobite *Hellraiser II*)

Steph Sciullo at Etsy:
https://www.etsy.com/shop/stephsciullo/
Average item review: 5 out of 5 stars (283)

Steph Sciullo on Instagram:
https://www.instagram.com/stephsciullo/

# ADRIAN BALDWIN – ILLUSTRATIONS

WINNER of INDIE NOVEL OF THE YEAR 2016 (Readers' Choice) at Underground Book Reviews.

Adrian Baldwin is a Mancunian now living and working in Wales. Back in the Nineties, he wrote for various TV shows/personalities: Smith & Jones, Clive Anderson, Brian Conley, Paul McKenna, Hale & Pace, Rory Bremner (and a few others). Wooo, get him.

Since then, he has written three screenplays, one of which received generous financial backing from the Film Agency for Wales. Then along came the global recession to kick the UK Film industry in the nuts. What a bummer!

Not to be outdone, he turned to novel writing - which had always been his real dream - and in particular, a genre he feels is often overlooked; a genre he has always been a fan of: Dark Comedy (sometimes referred to as Horror's weird cousin).

BARNACLE BRAT (a dark comedy for grown-ups), his first novel won Indie Novel of the Year 2016 award (see above) - his second novel STANLEY McCLOUD MUST DIE! (More dark comedy for grown-ups) published in 2016, and his third novel: THE SNOWMAN AND THE SCARECROW (another dark comedy for grown-ups) published in 2018.

Adrian Baldwin has also written several dark comedy short stories, some of which he has published himself, whilst others have appeared in anthologies published by a variety of indie publishers.

His latest solo project, DEVIL'S ACRE, is a horror/sci-fi/period drama; it's basically Victorians vs 'aliens' vs zombies! What's not to like. The unfolding story will be released in a series of novellas/novelettes – with Episode 1 The Great Stink already out there.

Besides this, Adrian has recently co-written a screenplay for A QUIET APOCALYPSE with Dave Jeffery, the author of the book of the same name.

Adrian cites his major influences as Kurt Vonnegut, Monty Python, Stephen King, David Bowie,

Christopher Moore, David Mitchell, Robert Rankin, Galton & Simpson, Colin Bateman, Bruce Robinson, Jasper Fforde and Irvine Welsh.

As of 2023/2024 Adrian decided to take a break from writing his weird novels and short stories to concentrate on creating new artworks. As the artist/author spent 4 years at art/technical college it's good to know those years weren't wasted! He says the drawings tend to be 'retro quirky' in a mix of ink and pencil. Adrian says he will sometimes take inspiration from old photos and postcards (Victorian/1950s/1960s/1970s) and reimagine them into something new. Some of his favourite drawings are those based on his dad's old photos - pure nostalgia. We look forward to seeing what he produces in the future.

For more information on the award-winning author, check out: www.adrianbaldwin.info (*You can read the beginnings of all his works there.)

# DEMAIN PUBLISHING

To keep up to-date on all news DEMAIN (including future submission calls and releases) you can follow us in a number of ways:

BLOG:
www.demainpublishingblog.weebly.com

TWITTER:
@DemainPubUk

FACEBOOK PAGE:
Demain Publishing

INSTAGRAM:
demainpublishing

# AUTHOR PHOTO CREDITS

Face: photo by Tim Dry

Background: photo by Robin Chaphkar

Cenobite Jewelry Photoshop: Barbie Wilde